BRIAN the DANCING LION

by Tom Tinn-Disbury

raintree
a Capstone company — publishers for children

For Mum, inside you're dancing. — TTD

Raintree is an imprint of Capstone Global Library Limited, a company incorporated in England and Wales having its registered office at 264 Banbury Road, Oxford, OX2 7DY – Registered company number: 6695582

www.raintree.co.uk
myorders@raintree.co.uk

Hardback edition text © Tom Tinn-Disbury 2023
Paperback edition text © Tom Tinn-Disbury 2024

ISBN 978 1 3982 3737 7 (hardback)
ISBN 978 1 3982 3738 4 (paperback)

Designed by Nathan Gassman
Printed and bound in India

British Library Cataloguing in Publication Data
A full catalogue record for this book is available from the British Library.

Brian **loved** to dance.

No matter the beat or the
rhythm, music made him move.

Dynamic disco music.

Calming classical music.

Funky soul music.

Dancing made Brian feel great, but he never told anyone.
Lions were meant to be brave and strong and fierce.
Nobody would think a dancing lion was brave or strong or fierce.

When his friends asked him,
"What will you be doing tonight, Brian?
Something strong and brave and fierce, no doubt."

Brian always replied the way they expected.

One morning, Brian was walking through the jungle when he came across a couple of gazelles dancing a cha-cha.

"What's all this?" he asked the gazelles.

"We're practising for the big dance competition," they replied. "Probably not a big, brave lion's cup of tea."

"Obviously," Brian hastily replied.
"What nonsense! Good day to you both!"

But he whispered to himself, "**This could be my chance!** If I can win, then maybe everyone will see that it's okay for lions to dance. Dancing lions are still brave and strong and fierce."

Brian practised day . . .

and night.

It was tricky having to keep such a big secret from his friends, but Brian imagined what would happen if they found out.

As the big competition approached, Brian was discussing techniques for being brave and strong and fierce with his friends. He could see other animals practising their dance routines, and he could hear the inspiring music.

Brian's foot started tapping.
Before he knew it, the beat had taken over.

Brian had gone into full-on **dance mode!**

Brian stopped.

He gave a small roar of embarrassment and ran
as fast as he could back to his den.

A few days passed, but Brian felt too miserable
and too embarrassed to see his friends.

He hid in his den.

Then, one day, he heard his friends outside calling to him.
Reluctantly, Brian opened the door.

Jim **loved** to stitch and sew,
designing fantastic clothes and costumes.

Betty **loved** crafting,
painting and building things.

And Barry **loved** to sing opera.

Brian was so relieved. He also felt a bit silly.
Surely he knew deep down that his friends would be happy for him.

That's what friends are for!

"I still missed the dance competition though," he sighed.

His friends all looked at each other and smiled.
"Yes, but we have an idea . . ."

The next evening, the four friends were proud to unveil their dance spectacular. And Brian danced.

His dance was **brave**
and **strong**
and **fierce**
and **beautiful.**

Just like him.